I'm a MONSTER TRUCK

By Dennis R. Shealy
Illustrated by Bob Staake

A GOLDEN BOOK • NEW YORK

Text copyright © 2011 by Dennis Shealy
Illustrations copyright © 2011 by Bob Staake
All rights reserved. Published in the United States by Golden Books, an imprint of Random House
Children's Books, a division of Random House, Inc., 1745 Broadway, New York, NY 10019.
Golden Books, A Golden Book, A Little Golden Book, the G colophon, and the distinctive gold spine
are registered trademarks of Random House, Inc.
www.randomhouse.com/kids
Educators and librarians, for a variety of teaching tools, visit us at www.randomhouse.com/teachers
Library of Congress Control Number: 2009940567
ISBN: 978-0-375-86132-1
Printed in the United States of America
10 9 8

To Diane, friend and editor
extraordinaire —D.S.

To Dade, a living,
breathing monster —B.S.

I smash!

I bash!

CRASH!

I love the sound
of breaking glass!

'Cause I'm a . . .

I was *made* to make mud fly.

I may slide, but I never slip.
My tall tires GRAB the dirt . . .

as I take tight twists
and extreme turns.

When I race, I race to win!

But racing isn't everything.
I'm gargantuan *and* graceful!
The freestyle event is where
I show off my smooth moves.

But heck, I *am* a monster truck.
And I love to crush cars under
my big wheels!

CRRRUNCH!

The more I crunch 'em,
the louder my fans cheer.

Uh-oh, looks like Carcharodontosaurus wants my leftovers. He's a monster machine that eats cars and breathes fire!

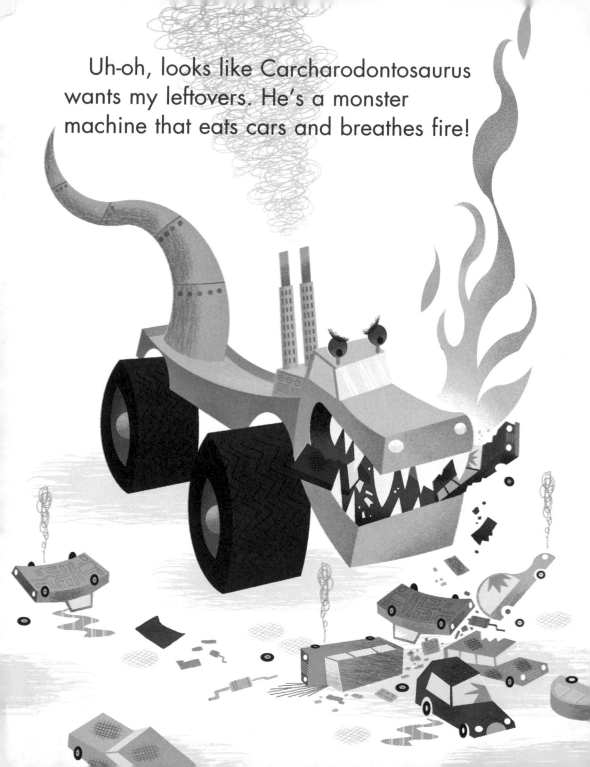

Don't worry—monster trucks aren't afraid of *anything*.

I'll put this mechanical menace back in his cage.

It's time for a break!
Let's watch the motorcycles take to the air.

They criss and they cross,
but they don't crash . . . .

and they do it all
without a net!

hang
time

There's my buddy Billy Wrecks. He and his crew are part of the demolition derby.

They smash, bash, and crash each other until there's only one car left in the mud.

But don't worry—
they love it!

When the show's over,
we love to take one last
lap for the crowd.